The Endless Machine

Max Ingram

Copyright © 2015 Max Ingram

Published by Bone Forge Books

ISBN: 0692327649
ISBN-13: 978-0692327647

CONTENTS

The Voyage

Man of Excess

ACKNOWLEDGMENTS

Cover art by Ryan Wardlow.
You can learn more about this artist and view samples of
his work at www.artofryanwardlow.weebly.com

~ CHAPTER ONE ~
THE VOYAGE

Diaspora

The earth itself bellowed in protest,
shuddering like a wooden dock fit
hard, the beaching of this black,
fiery behemoth, leaving a carver's
mark miles long. And the great fish
lay, her metal ribs rippling beneath
this new world's strain, unaccustomed to
such vaporous pressures.

Her skin; broken, scarred and pocked,
belied the beauty she remembered,
the elegance she held dear. It shamed her,
to be spread flat and fixed
on this ugly, teaming rock, her flanks
bulging from the weight of being
tossed from her sea; environs far lighter,
far more graceful than this
intended for her passage.

Her mouth was made for the swallowing
of lives, the ingestion of doomed legacy.
Her great teeth, to strain through the flotsam
presented, picking out the liveliest krill to
consume. Then keeping them curled and
gestate in her belly, both mother and devourer
to her prey.

Continued...

She could feel them unfurling, their eager
lives churning beneath her failing skin,
eating away at her remaining flesh, her
very dissection serving to nourish their birth.

And to this world they would spill, wet-eyed
and naked to the rain, innocent in their newly
born knowledge. No remnants of their
apocalyptic ways. And she, their nursemaid of
fire, metal and – ultimately – love, would be
consumed by the elements, the days of
hard-sought rain, mud slicks and summer dry
desiccation. But her children's children would
remember her stripped iron ribs reaching for
home.

Death Artifact

It hunches, prone upon the earth, its
fetal-shaped forelimbs being
swallowed by sand, by greedy earth
gone too long hungry for rain, for life,
for anything. The wind beating against its
pale, chitinous hide, scraping its
reddened sores raw; spreading their
flesh-gaping infections.

The very spine of it groans, whimpering
as the shifting gusts of wind tug upon it,
unforgiving. Its face is broken, misshapen,
teeth pulled whole from its blackened
gums, bile-like saliva spilling over its
sunken chin.

If not dead, it is near death and wishing for
any hand to push it that one, fearful step
off. I nudge its hardened hide with the
toe of my boot, and hear the shell of it
clank in response. A foul odor leaks
from its belly, a stinging fume that brings
mist to my eyes.

Continued...

And I notice, oddly, that
some fool has affixed a brand upon its
half-sunk, defeated haunches. A series
of numbers, a jumble of letters, in a
foreign tongue my people have yet to
decipher in full.

I wonder if all of them ended
in similar fashion. The roving beasts
of this world. Affixed to the earth and
rotting of indecision.

First Contact

A fly in my face, dipping
darting, trying for any
chance at touching my
skin, at landing, at licking
my cheeks with its tongue
distended and spittle-slick.

My barn-like hands buffet
the wind, slapping at air
and always missing the
circus performer of
six-legged fame, still
undefeated.

But when I do chance to
crush his little form; my
hand, the table, smeared
of his broken-wide thorax and
spilled, paste-like innards,
I look at that remnant and
begin to wonder.

Continued...

Did he seek me out, did
he choose me, for my
flesh, my flavor, the scent
of my body on the air. Or
did he instead, find me
an attraction by other
measures, and in his own
strange and alien way
want love?

Gramuth Rising

We had known fear in the face of oblivion,
in the whispered recriminations of old men
suddenly wise, and the free falling tears
of our mothers. But never this. Never yet
here.

Never with smooth hands clenched to
cramping, 'round rough-carved sticks
in the face of mountainous gods, booming
their guileless blood-songs, tongues slick
with the faces of our families.

They were angered by our falling, our
blackening of their fields, our arrogant,
thin-limbed preening and powdered
cheeks in the harsh, jungle swelt.

We thought they were storms, or maybe
earthquakes, shaking the world and the
heavens by throat, until we saw. We saw
the Gramuth rising, from miles away as it was
the only means. Up close they were simply
everything.

Aerosol Tight

The captain was a crisp and white-smocked
man, born on paradisiac plains where even
insects were harnessed for ploughing. His
mustachioed mirth was often called into service
on the long, powdered, puffed-up drift from one
galactic pond to another. And even the gabbering
dames of Delphic, oracular gesticulations could
not help but sway silent in the musk of his
presence.

But once here, once landed and dock-side the
dapper must diminish. For the swelt was
too much, and the insects were wild, in ways that
not even a moon camp could have hinted. And
the Delphic dames were unable to soar in their
flotsam projectors, stuck fast to the earth and
mud-bound for the first time since they elected to
forgo such pubescent endeavors.

Our Dzu-Teh, impetuous and flabbergasting as
always, took to the trees like a gibbering horde,
shaking the fruit-stuffs and flatulent globs like
birthing day fire bobbles. You would think they
had never had freedom, despite the rather long
leashes employed.

And it took several sharp jabbings and
shockings most dire to garner their
obeisance, dragging them somber and dejected
to earth.

Once there, we beat them, quite rightly,
quite sound, and set about the installing of
humming cords and toilets - lighted, and
aerosol tight.

A Quiet Exchange

Cora watches from her
windswept perch, on the
cliffside overlooking the
valley below, her taut belly
flattened on the fertile tract,
girded by a gun belt and
breathing slow.

Herdsmen hunker on the
backs of blunt-nosed Golas,
the bow-legged creatures bay
and click, and circled in the middle
are the mass of Dzu-Teh,
round-eyed and running with
shoulders sweat-slick.

Bred from the born-frees and
borrowed from nature, they were
not natural in themselves,
so the high-born Sodality in their
all-knowing modality
declared the Dzu-Teh as patented
and shelved.

Cora aims along her rifle's
neck, its nose resting on boulders,
as quiet puffs of air belch forth,
light lancing deadly, clipping the
heads of herdsmen off shoulders.

The Dzu-Teh shudder, jaws
swinging wide, as they hunch
and cluster in hairy swells, like
speckled moles on a man's back.

On sight of Cora, as she
scrambles down and jogs to
join them, they lift their blunted skulls
and whimper, mouthing their hope
for salvation in guttural moans, the
backs of their five-fingered paws offered,
wrists lashed in plasti-straps and
eager to be free.

But on drawing close, Cora pulls her
pistol and levels it, a grin spreading
on her austere cheeks, her green
eyes glitter with the banknotes she
can already see in their bruised faces.

Wormholes

Birds bolt loose from the canopy, like a
cluster grenade gone wide, their own small
limbs trembling in transit, with the branches
woken, bleary-eyed, left behind. Then silence.

The green top rolls, languid as ocean swells,
while beneath its tree-propped waves,
a silent cacophony of thunderous heartbeats
are held in check, ears twitched, propped,
swiveled; listening for that hair-stiffening cry.
The wail that wounded their ears and
frightened them in the first.

Then it comes. Mournful, low and shuddering.
Wet-lipped agony expressed without tongue,
without language, or any known word that
we would call bestial or man.

The figure is horror-formed and flat upon
the earth, dragging itself through the
underbrush, the sky-shrouding canopy
looms like a mother distraught, watching
wet-eyed, her newly born child of deformity.

The silence persists. No creature here
knowing what to make of this blind, groping,
wailing thing.

Its hind legs are sheared at mid-thigh,
squirting browns, reds and yellows
across the leaves and twigs behind it like
expressionist arrogance.

Its fat, smacking lips gape and close,
snapping at the air as though tasting it
for the first, chewing it toothless, gumming
each atmospheric mouthful with
throat-shuddering consequence, the
sides of its smooth, hairless, damp face
belching outward, shaking of spasms,
showing their disfavor for this meal.

And amid the trees behind it, slicing
equally through bark, stone and bloodied
forest floor remains, shivers and dances
eagerly the dervish-hole in the daylight.
Its aperture leading to a damp, soil-shored
expanse of strangely colored, stone-pocked
tunnels. Violet, trailing gases seeping out like
a punctured bicycle tire.

It winks; once, twice, pausing for moments
between slicing at the wind passing through it,
a door of razor-wire reality that has no more
kindness for its wounded, dirt-born traveler than
for an atom, a molecule, or the clipped wings
of a fly.

The Endless Machine I:
The Voyage

I take the railing like I would a
lover's hand, leaning forward, washing
my face in stars. An angel's halo rings
my neck, a noose of timid light, and I stand,
observing, praying upon the altar of
God's unwritten word, his scriptures
sketched in flight.

I sail upon this
blackest of all oceans, which no man
knows whither the roots of it run.

A silver, lancing arrow that splits
the forests my fathers feared. I have
named it. It is mine. I ride upon it and
stab it through my ribs, as I must, so that
I may bleed.

It is only when
wounded by my vessel, penetrated by its
razor nose and lifted on high, beyond all
reckonings or compasses, that I may reach,
fingers cramping, straining, tendons
over-extended and popping like dried
seed husks. For though there is
only darkness to my eyes, I know it
holds more.

The Endless Machine II:
She is Mine

From my seat upon high, awash in
shattered remnants of swollen, weeping
stars and stumbling, wayward planets, I
gaze upon none of them. My eyes are
riveted more distant, swiveling like
spotlights on a prison beach, bordering
waters too black, too vast to traverse.
But I dare to regardless.

She is old, and her bones of ore groan
ceaselessly, weighed down by the
oppression of endless night. But I can
see her gentle spark, her lambent spirit,
her soul which remembers its youth, the
feeling of grass beneath her iron heels and
cloud-filled skies crowning her brow, making
a holly wreath for celebration.

It was the day she was born, the day she
was christened as "Lezna" and adored by
millions. Her Spanish maker gave his soul in
the effort. And he watched in graveborn silence
on a hilltop, as she first awoke. Now, she is
adored by only me, while those millions
lie buried and scattered, feeding the
endless machine.

Continued...

She hums beneath my hands, warming
to my touch, her dials lighting as she smiles.
It is I who guide her to stretch, in languid,
pregnant pauses amid the expanse. She
permits me, in cradled warmth, to vault
galaxies while clinging to her glorious,
burnished breast.

I would be jealous should a single soul
but mine set foot upon her flooring.
So we never speak of those who once
walked her, of those who died, gasping,
faces blanched and turgid, within her walls.

The Endless Machine III:
In Time

There are many who sleep, but I alone
stand waking, charged in my
sacred watch. I bear a timepiece as
rough and aged as the words I curl
my tongue around. It is ever-present
at my hip. Ticking in its
reliable rhythm, setting the cadence
of days, of weeks, of stretching,
yawning existence.

In time we came to speak, to
listen to one another. She murmured
beneath floorboards, gentle sighs
accompanied each course change,
with my hands upon her consoles. Her
pulse bled through fingers frayed at the
ends of my arms. Her eyes
accompanied me, always.

Her voice was... lyrical. Like a
softly chanted tribal song. A lullaby
spoken by mothers in darkness, with
only the cracked open door to show
light at all.

Continued...

We are to be married, she and I, made
union most holy and perfect, our
spirits fused, of flesh and glowing ore.

The sun will be our pastor. He will
join us and we shall exult in his light,
as one, and then, blessedly, no more.

My Fall

I hurtled, arcing,
brain knocked black,
limbs splayed wild
like a broken, half-strung
marionette.

I felt nothing, saw nothing, slept
like a bottle-rich drunkard in my
skin of motley hues.

Cast out from the gates of my
father's house. Another argument.
Just as stupid, just as pointless as
all the rest. I don't know why we
keep going 'round. He's always
disappointed. I'm always
angry.

Then he gets
angry too, and we fight. But
his fists are always bigger, his reach
more substantial than mine.

So here I am.
A light in the morning sky, a
rainbow of broken ice clouds and
vapor tracks, my head bowed in a
semblance of silent respect that I
would only show while unconscious.

Continued...

Thermosphere, Mesosphere...

My iron-gray skin begins to
glow, rubbed raw by thickening
gasses, my body tossing in
torrential, blasting winds that no
living soul could stand.

I fall.

Statosphere, Troposphere...

A silent, cloud-torn line ending in
a dust bomb explosion, the earth burst
wide as a wound in my wake. A crater.
A cradle, where I lay in fetal
posture, awaiting my name.

And they will have one.
They will have many, but they will
always remember my fall.

~ CHAPTER TWO ~
MAN OF EXCESS

Moon Party
(for Amy)

The children spill from their
car-sized capsule like
granules of aspirin gone wide,
tiny bodies of
torrential laughter and
giddy-grinned mischief all
bundled together by
combs and a
caring mother's kiss.

They flow between our toes and
over our ankles
like rivulets of water in flood,
but our eyes are far more fixed
upon a moon which, apparently,
forgot to arrive.

We use the darkness to
indemnify,
to surround our faces in
fire-lit hush, as we
gaze gape-mouthed at the
burgeoning blanket of
prognosticated sky.

Continued...

Wondering,
as people are wont to do,
whether the
chicken gizzard gazing of
weathermen will
deliver us from all evil.

Did You See What He Said?

He shoves the book hard against her
waiting hands. He grins, red-faced, eyebrows
rampant in their attempt to climb his head.
"*Read it,*" he says. "*Read that part,*" he wheezes,
finger prodding the page.

And she recites, not yet
sure of the joke. Not yet
sure of the implication. Pausing as she
works her lips over new words, not yet
sure where they might take her. Before long
she stops, mouthing the remainder in
side-glancing silence.

"*Did you see it?*"
His finger jabs, poking hard on the page.
"*He says 'Fucking my fist!' Can you believe that?!*"
Then laughs so hard he loses all
sign of humanity.

"*This is...*" she pauses, uncomfortable "*...sad.*"
She blinks, uncertain of her footing.
"*He's talking about...*" she shrugs "*...being sad.
Being desperate.*"

Continued...

"*But did you see?*"
He smacks the page, wondering why she
doesn't laugh.
"*Did you see what he said?*"
Then he grabs the book with a
disinterested snort and tries to
find someone with a
sense of humor.

Dead People

The pills tend to
rattle against my
ferryboat gums,
those
fleshy planks which
pull words between them with
hatred normally reserved
for food,
as though
every swallow might be the
one to kill me.

I lick the tips of those
chemical matches I find,
phosphorous and sulfur
immolate my lies,
and my lantern jaw
gapes and distends,
sending flickers of light on
dead frequencies.

I'm useless now with no
seeds or sons or
silly photos of
Christmas sweaters wrapping
dead people in bows.

Merry Christmas

Gave me a fistful of
murdered dreams,
death still fresh on their
frozen smiles,
and all I could wish for were my
two front teeth;
like Christmas,
selfish and sad.

Had to make a choice between
'Crazy Max' and *'Fun Max'*
never knowing
which was truly which,
never sure if
anything mattered beyond just
betting on percentages of sanity.

I flushed 'em down the toilet,
each pill like a
pearl-white sacrifice to some
waterlogged god,
and the dreams came back
floating and film-covered in sewage,
but we're
getting re-acquainted.

Desert Demon

The usurper king
in all his
detritus,
demi-god-like glory,
clothed in the remnants of
gods turned ash
and religions reigning for
countless millennia before
shattering as glass.

He is the
great, gape-mawed
devourer,
tongue slavering over
blood in repose.

His grinding jaw is
thunder loosed amid
mountains trembling,
clouds set boiling and
the heavens wracked in
shame.

Continued...

The wind bemoans in
protest;
unheard,
unheeded and
ignored,
as one flesh devours
all flesh,
leaving blood as wine
on the butcher's floor.

Zombie and Moon

(for Mary Beth)

Like Zombie and Moon,
two blood-wet souls in the
black;
shivering in showers of
lightning borne lungs that
scream,
sob,
and shudder
for the rack.

They grind their
inconstant flesh,
their magnet-locked
insanities,
sensing like
wounded pups by
smell,
touch and
taste of blood, that
each one is wounded and
searching for the other.

Thousand-fold Colour
(for Maria)

I emerge from my blankets
as a rolling wave,
throwing off the deep blues of
my coverlet and
rising naked,
awake,
like foam and water
transformed to a
more ephemeral state,
ready to climb the shoreline.

I walk to your
body, your shape,
your significant nakedness,
offered
sacrificial-style on the
planks of my desk,
a barely breathing reminder
of power,
of sex and
love poems written
loop-form in my cum.

You're arrayed like a tray;
flesh, warm and pale,
limbs imbued with the
etchings of Sun.

My fingers slip along the
well-traveled canal,
the devil-sweet dip,
the Euphrates made
flesh between
your tightly snug thighs.

There is
a syrup to find;
shining sweet gold on the
pads of my fingers.
I wet my lips with your
engulfing grace,
paint my tongue in its
thousand-fold colour and
devour you whole.

I am a Man of Excess

I am a
man of excess, a
misanthrope staring
hard-fisted at the
fires of man.

Wrapped in robes of
bitter insanity, dubbed
too sane to make any
kind of sense.

I am the
matchstick of rampant,
screaming profanity,
lighting torches in the fists of
village idiots amassing to
burn me alive.

And the cruelest
joke of all is that
I was made to be a poet but
not even a good one.

The Footpath Widens

Perched upon the
precipice of a
black-skied purgatory,
my fists and toes taking
purchase of the earth,
mud-wet and
misanthropic in their
defiance.

I gaze
wet-bearded at the blackness,
my teeth the only thunder,
my eyes the white of
lightning struck;
my face,
a cliffside of
shattered admonitions, like
broken spears left jutting,
half-rotted and forgetful of
the hands that threw them.

Building fires in the black,
wet sticks my only tender,
choking on the
smoking remains of
sacrificed sons split
wide and deaf.

Continued...

Blood,
my only bargaining chip,
black and clotted of death,
disease lacing its
every coursing tendril and
I spill it,
as limbs left tumbling on
the jungle floor,
carving great trenches of
regret in my flesh;
passages for the
purification of a
soul I don't deserve.

Broken

Split wide and
wounded by
God knows what,
the tree looked
sad
from here.

Its twin trunks cut,
carved by lightning and
spread-eagle,
like an alley-corpse
post raping.

Skin black and
blistered, I was
sure it was dead
from a distance.

But closer I could
see it was green in
unexpected places.

I realized, grazing its
scarred husk of flesh,
that its body was
broken,
but somehow
still growing.

ABOUT THE AUTHOR

Max Ingram is an author and poet from the arid climes of Arizona. He has always loved the bizarre, strange and fantastic, immersing himself in comic books, video games and Sci-Fi/horror films from a young age. The Endless Machine is his second collection of poetry.